Collection of Short Stories and Poems II

Mary Martin

Rainbows

Two little rainbows in the sky
they shined down low
and they shined up high
the rain went away and
the sun shone bright
two little rainbows said goodbye.

Wild Turkeys

Turkeys, wild turkeys
strutting their stuff
please don't disturb them,
or stir up their fluff.
Thanksgiving is coming,
oh turkey dear.
those turkeys, wild turkeys are my pets
don't you see--and are so dear to me.

Autumn

The autumn air has a calming effect
caressing my skin
The garden is full and the mums
 are bright and beautiful
The flowers smell sweet with
the fragrance they give.
Nature's perfume overwhelms my
senses
with ecstasy.

Red, yellow, purple
all in a green background
trees bold and strong
leaves yellow, brown, and gold,
apples mature and ripe

pleasing to pick.
Autumn is here,
my favorite time of year.

Prey
The day turns into night
with eventual moon rise.
The kitten arises from where
it was curled up in a fluff of
black and white.
He stretches and yawns ~~
another night to prowl around
on the farm
An owl screeches, hunting its prey,
but not tonight old owl.
The kitten reigns victorious from the
owl,
his mouse got away.
But the clever kitten knows his prey…

the mouse did *not* get away.

To Nadine

We went walking down the lane
barefoot, walking hand in hand
we saw the birdies playing in the
puddles
we said, "Why not?" and joined the fun
in the muddy puddles.

We sang, laughed, and ran playing from
early morn 'til end of day.
We only stopped to eat our lunch,
then away we flew like a thrush.

I've loved you then,
I love you still,

how sweet you are,
my Kentucky girl.

Mini Stories

~*~

Cowboy I

Long ago there lived a cowboy. One day, he set out riding and rode across the prairie, slow over the canyon. He rode from sunup to sundown, the ridges high and valleys low. He then got tired of riding and crossed a river wide. He wished upon a star which led him back to me.

Cowboy II

Along the western plain, a cowboy swept in low and lean. They never knew for certain his name, but people called him Jimmy. He was mighty mean. They took his wife and daughter, murdered before his very eyes. His wife, a southern beauty, with sweetness in her smile. They lived and loved together 'til they met their demise. The cowboy rides alone, revenge now in his eyes.

Cowboy III

The cowboy and the Indian fought a fearful battle, but neither of them won. Cowboys, Indians, and horses all around. They both died on the battlefield. One went to heaven, the other to the happy hunting ground.

Short Stories

Cassie

The water drops beat against the panes of the apartment window. Cassie awakened to a new spring day. Cassie could hear Mom and Dad talking in the kitchen.

"Now, I told you. We can't afford a new

car this year, Alice," stormed her father.
"But Robert, the Volkswagen is too small now," countered her mother.
The old car was in need of repair.
"By the time we fix the Volkswagen, we could put a down payment on a new car," Alice said.
"I have to go to work," replied Robert.
"We'll talk about this later."
Cassie dressed and walked to school. All day she thought of what to buy her mother for her birthday. She already spent her allowance so she couldn't buy a present. Finally, she decided to bake a cake. When Cassie came home, her Dad asked her to watch Elizabeth and Rob. It was a Thursday. On the first Thursday of every month the tenants had an apartment meeting in the

basement. Mom was at the meeting now. It was also Mom's birthday. Cassie hurried to make Mom's cake. Dad came home and they waited for the meeting to end.

Around six with supper over and the dishes washed, Cassie set the table. The cake was placed in the center. A small group of friends and relatives came in and out to wish Mom a Happy Birthday. Then Dad took Mom downstairs. When they reached the garage, Mom looked at the new car Dad bought for her. She was so happy, she cried. However, the next day would be devastating.

When Cassie came home from school, her mother told her Dad died of a heart attack. Many people came to the funeral, and Mom was heartbroken. Her parents had a lot of friends who brought over casseroles and warm condolences. Cassie felt sick and clung to her mother for fear of losing her too. Three days later Mom said they were moving to Tennessee because working on a farm was all that Mom knew how to do.

~*~

Arriving

Cassie looked down the long, winding road with anxiety. The school bus would arrive soon. For the first time, Cassie didn't want to go to school. In the city Cassie always walked to school. Two blocks of neighbors waving and smells of Mrs. Hansen's yeast rolls would always filter through the morning air. "The city is alive. It is the best place in the world," Dad used to say.

The long trail of dust coming down the road interrupted Cassie's thoughts. The bus came to a stop. Cassie sighed as she boarded. She sat in the front seat… alone. When the bus arrived at the third stop, Cassie noticed that only smaller children were boarding. But as it neared the city, children of different ages also got on.

Oh, great! Cassie thought. *Here I am in the boondocks, and only one kid my age lives near me. Well, it did have to be a boy! Ugh! I wish Mom had never grown up on a farm. I wouldn't be in this mess now.*

The bus climbed a hill and stopped just short of a curve, and a little girl with pigtails got on. She sat down beside Cassie.

"Hi, I'm Millie, what's your name?" she asked all in one breath.

"Cassie Dunwin," replied Cassie evenly as Millie started to twist and turn in her seat.

"Hey Millie, sit still!" Cassie snapped. Millie sat silently for a few seconds, and Cassie thought she saw tears in her eyes.

"Look Millie, I'm sorry. What's your last name?" she asked.

"Millie Morgan, but most people call me M&M."

"M&M...why? That's so ditsy!"

"My first and last names begin with the letter M, and I like the candy. People are always giving me M&M's. I like it, it's neat!" Millie said.

Cassie remembered all the stories Mom had told to her about Kentucky.

"Folks are always giving you things down there…and the flowers are so wonderful. There are fields of flowers, bigger than Sander's greenhouse." Her mother's voice echoed through her memory. Cassie always thought they were just stories.

"Cassie, what does ditzy mean?" Millie asked.

Cassie crossed her legs and said, "Never mind, Millie." She didn't want to hurt Millie by telling her it meant silly. She reminded her of Elizabeth.

Elizabeth Dunwin was five and full of questions. She could talk a tick off a dog. She made up her own jokes, too! "Cassie, I'm six. I have one brother. He is four, his name is Steve. I'm in the first grade at Greyson Elementary School. Will you tell me about you?" Millie asked.

Yeah, she's like Elizabeth, Cassie thought.

"Well I'm 10 and I'll be starting the fifth grade. My sister's name is Elizabeth, she's five, and I have one brother named Robert who's four. My mother's name is Mrs. Alice Dunwin," explained Cassie.

"My mom's name is Betty and dad's is Billy. What does your dad do?" she asked.

"Mine's dead, and I don't want to talk about it. What's yours do?" Cassie asked, pushing back tears.

"He's working at The Down Home Supermarket, but he's saving to buy some land."

The bus made its last trek down the road and crossed the railroad tracks, finally climbing up the hill.

"Oh Cassie I gotta go. I'll see you later," said Millie as she got up and left the bus. Her brown pig tails bobbed against her neck as she walked happily to the Greyson Elementary School. Cassie got off and went straight to the principal's office. There she found a middle aged woman who wore cat eye glasses, peering at her from behind a stack of manila folders.

"Hi, I'm Cassie Dunwin and I'm…" began Cassie.

"You're Alice Whalen's daughter. I'm glad to meet you, Cassie. I'm Mrs. Mullens, the school secretary. You will be starting with Mrs. Smith in the fifth grade. Go down the hall to room 211, and I'll let Mrs. Smith know you are here," explained the woman.

Cassie was afraid so she went to the water fountain. As she raised her head, she could see Mrs. Mullens's face. She looked at Cassie sternly.

"Cassie, don't just stand there, *go to your room!*" she said.

Cassie swallowed hard and turned to go to her room, but as she reached the door, she looked back. Mrs. Mullens had been watching to see if she would go to the room. Cassie knocked hard on the door.

"Yes?" she asked.

"I'm Cassie Dunwin," she said when a tall woman opened the door.

"Oh, little Cassie Dunwin! Come in! I need to ask you some questions."

Oh no, thought Cassie. *It's Elizabeth all grown up.*

Mrs. Smith looked just like Elizabeth, with her sweet face and tumbly brown hair.

"Class," Mrs. Smith began, "This is Cassie Whal…I mean Cassie Dunwin. She has moved here from New York City."

Cassie felt like crawling underneath the teacher's desk. Mrs. Smith almost said Cassie *Whalen,* and the kids looked at her like she was in a Halloween costume as she sat down in the front now.

The girls wore jeans and lacy blouses, while the boys's attire was a simple button down shirt, and jeans as well. Cassie had on her favorite shirt with holes down the back, her blue jean mini skirt and a pair of vintage tennis shoes. She teased her hair until it was big and poofy.

The boy behind her said, "Ain't it little Miss Hollywood!" Everyone laughed, except for Mrs. Smith.

"John Lewis, go to the office, and I'll be there shortly!"

To everyone else she said, "Class, I'll be right back. Mrs. Kearns will be looking after you." She then turned and walked to the office.

The kids were pretty upset, and Cassie was blamed because John was sent to the office.

Class went on as usual when Mrs. Smith came back. She was nice to Cassie, but it was plain to see the class haden't accepted her. She tried to talk to the girl beside her but her friend said that John wouldn't like it, so she turned away from Cassie.

At lunch, John Lewis was allowed to join the class again. He didn't even speak to the other kids. Cassie got her tray and sat beside Tommy who decided to get up and move. She tried to sit beside Becky who did the same. She noticed John Lewis sitting by himself.

I wonder what Dad would do? I know what Mom would say--'You have to be strong within,' Cassie thought to herself.

Cassie got up and walked right up to John and sat down beside him. He pretended not to notice her.

"Look John Lewis, I'll trade you my dessert for your peas," Cassie said. Cassie hated peas but if he'd talk, it would be worth the trade.

"Sure!" said John as they traded.

Cassie asked, "John, why don't you like me?"

John replied, "Er…I…uh…well, you look funny."

Cassie said, "You'd dress funny too if you lived in New York City and wore that."

"Hey," John said, "That's not funny."
"John, your joke about Miss Hollywood wasn't funny either."
"I know. I'll try to be nicer. Pals?" John asked.
He looked at her and put out his hand for her to shake.
I guess it's as close to an apology as he can come, Cassie thought.
"Sure, pals," she said, shaking his hand. When the day resumed, it went a lot better, and the class began to accept her.
Mrs. Smith said that she had to bring a paper sack for her new book. The bell rang and Cassie went off to the bus. There on the front seat was Millie waiting for her. Cassie sat down and Millie said, "Why didn't you tell me?"

"Tell you what?" Cassie asked.

"That you're *her*," said Millie.

"Who?" asked Cassie.

"Cassie Whalen," said Millie.

"I'm not! I'm Cassie Dunwin," she insisted.

"You're Alice Walen's daughter, aren't you?" asked Millie.

"That's what my mom's last name was," replied Cassie.

"Oh, wow!" said Millie.

***

Cassie was tired when she got home, and she didn't even notice the difference. But when her mom drove up, she noticed a run-down station wagon. She ran outside and her mom got out with Elizabeth and Robert.

"Mom, where's our car?" she asked.

"Cassie, I had to trade it in," Mom said.

"But Mom, you can't! Dad gave you that car," said Cassie.

"Cassie, we won't need it here," said mom. "I traded it for this car and a used tractor."

"But Mom!" Cassie continued.

"Cassie, get the groceries inside the house, and be strong within," replied her mother.

Then she looked at Elizabeth and Robert, and back at Cassie.

Cassie knew what mom meant, and she knew in her heart how much Elizabeth and Robert needed them both now more than ever before. So, Cassie helped Mom run the house just like Dad knew she could.

***

It had been 12 years since Alice Dunwin had driven a tractor, and it was hard work. However, she remembered how to drive safely and how to perform maintenance as needed. Mrs. Dunwin knew all the safety rules, but taking care of a tractor could be expensive. Maybe if old Mr. Hines lived somewhere nearby, she could call him for major repairs.

She remembered as a girl how old Mr. Hines moved around a lot so she needed to ask at the Post Office if he still lived around here. All of this was new to the children. Robert Jr. and Elizabeth were young, they would adapt to life on the farm she knew. But Cassie was the one who would have to learn all over again. City rules did not apply here.

Mrs. Dunwin took time to teach her eldest daughter each day. Sometimes supper was late, or the dishes would go undone until the next day. Cassie learned quickly and watched carefully. She asked only if she did not understand how to do something, Mother and daughter were inseparable until Cassie learned enough to do things alone. Elizabeth and Robert had been taken to Mrs. Ginger White's house. Ginger and Alice went to school together, and were best friends. When Alice heard Ginger was her next door neighbor, she decided to pay her a call. Ginger and Alice picked up their old friendship like they had never been apart. Alice told Ginger how she planned to teach Cassie how to plant, weed, and transplant tobacco. Ginger asked Alice about Beth and Rob. Alice said she had not planned that yet, but she was sure something would work out.

Ginger offered to watch her two younger children while she was busy. Alice replied, "Yes, Ginger. Thank you so much!"

She then took Robert and Elizabeth to Ginger's just after Cassie got home. Cassie changed her clothes, and made a sandwich before doing what homework she could finish while Mom was gone. When Mom returned, the books were put away, and they started to work on whatever needed to be done. They bought seed and began to plant tobacco. As evening fell and it became too dark to see, Mom washed her hands and drove off to pick up Robert and Elizabeth.

If there was time, the dishes were done along with some other light housework. Then, Cassie took a shower, dressed for bed, and laid out her clothes for school. Mom showered and dressed for bed as well. She checked the doors, windows, lights, and made sure all the children were covered up. Then, she went to bed.

5am

That was wake-up time.

"Cassie," said her mother, "You get 30 minutes to get ready. After that, I need you downstairs with me."

Cassie dressed, made her bed, and combed her hair. She only spent five minutes on her hair, no more than that. Cassie didn't need to go through a fuss now that she stopped teasing her hair. She let it fall down her back straight like the girls at school did. Sometimes, she put ribbons or ponytails in her hair, but she kept it simple.

She kept an organized list of duties, and which days and times they needed to get done.

Monday~~Clear out all paper.

Tuesday~~Straighten dresser, top to bottom.

Wednesday~~Clean closet.

Thursday~~Clean beneath bed.

Friday~~Dust, and wash bed blankets.

Saturday~~Take rugs out and shake, sweep, mop.

Casssie had two hours to herself on Sunday and her room was finished. This is where Monday's paper came from-- she wrote, drew, and played games from things she crafted out of paper. When she cleaned on Monday, the trash can was filled to the brim of paper. There was so very much homework, so the dresser top became a wasteland of erasers, ink pens, pencils, a ruler, a dictionary, hair accessories, and yarn. So on Tuesday, she would straighten it up again.

Wednesday they usually had math homework, and she organized her closet Thursday--no homework. She cleaned underneath the bed sometimes, for she would drop things and didn't have time to pick them up when they'd slide off. Friday--she had crafts to do, so she dusted and got a clean scarf for the dresser top. When Saturday came, all major cleaning was done. Not only in her room, but in the house as well. She helped with laundry, sweeping, mopping, dusting, and cleaning the kitchen.

Mom and Cassie weeded the tobacco beds and sprayed them.

"We'll have to hire people to pull plants, cut, and house the tobacco. When we sell the crop I plan to buy some chickens and a milk cow. Eggs are a good income here, and a cow is easier on the budget than buying milk, cream, and butter," explained her mother.

Cassie didn't know anything about chickens or a cow.

Mom explained to her over and over again how to feed the chickens and the cow, how to gather the eggs and the milk as well. Explaining wasn't enough, and Mom knew it. So, she let Cassie spend one night every other week with friends and neighbors to learn how to collect milk and gather eggs. Cassie also came to understand how to milk the cow, as well to churn and separate cream to make butter. She was able to gleam further knowledge of life on a farm, like not allowing the calf in with its mother when being weaned.

Mrs. Harris was the town's best quilter, and she promised to instruct Cassie. Amy Summers taught Cassie how to knit.

Miss Summers said, "It's not easy at first--you kinda feel like you're all thumbs."

It took three months for Cassie to grasp these different hobbies. Afterwards, Miss Summers showed her how to make sweaters, blankets, socks, and even vests.

Mr. Arnold had a beautiful garden started, and he showed Cassie about gardening. Cassie's head and back ached from weeding the tobacco plants. She would begin learning how to pull them soon. She asked her mother about planting a garden of their own.

Mom said, "Not this year Cassie, but perhaps next year."

"But Mom, I know how to. All..." she

began.

"Cassie!" Mom said sternly. "Not this year!"

Cassie was hurt, but she knew not to ask more than once. Later Mom came to her and said, "Cassie, we don't have the money to seed for a garden."

She cried and her mother said, " You must be strong within."

***

By harvest time, Cassie knew that caring for her sister and brother was her responsibility. Mom had Mr. Harris take the grain to market, and he got a fair price. Mom sat Cassie down and explained to her that part of the money would be put in the bank. The rest they would live on until next spring planting came again. She had bought a few things for the children and put them up until Christmas.

Cassie's first Christmas on the farm was very different than Christmas in the city. She used to get odd jobs in the city to buy Christmas presents with. Here in the middle of nowhere, she hadn't any idea of what to do to buy presents with. She had been working at a quilt, and was nearly finished.

Miss White had called to ask if they were going to the Country Days Fair. She told Cassie all about it and explained that if you had something to trade, you set up a trading table. If you had something to sell, you set up a table which said sell.

Cassie spent most of her spare time

finishing the quilt. When Country Days came, Mom set up a table for selling. They had cakes, pies, apples, and the quilt Cassie made. At the conclusion of the fair, Cassie's quilt went for over fifty dollars. This meant that Cassie would spend ten dollars for each person in the family for Christmas. She learned how to make crafts at school in art class. The remaining twenty dollars was spent buying materials.

Christmas evening came, and Cassie gave her gifts out. Mrs. White received a satin and lace umbrella Cassie had made, Mr. and Mrs. Harris received a bill box with four sections; bills paid, purchased items, bills due, and misc. Mr. Harris was so pleased now they could keep track of the bills.

Before school had let out, Cassie gave Mrs. Smith an apple which read *No. 1 Teacher.* She set the apple upon her desk, where it remained until the end of the school year. Christmas day came and Cassie gave her mother a bottle of perfume. Elizabeth received a crying doll, and Rob loved his new toy tractor.

Cassie received a lot of wonderful gifts, but the one that was her favorite was Old Black the horse from Mr. and Mrs. Harris. Cassie spent a lot of time with Old Black, but she also had the children to babysit. She grew into a beautiful woman and raised three strong children of her own. Cassie never forgot what her mother always said--*Cassie, you must be strong within.*

The Friendship

Dedicated to my editor
Owl Willows

Bill, Tim. and Keith worked at the Rockwood Plastic Plant. Every year in April, the plant shuts down. They took that time to clean and repair machines--just general maintenance.

Bill and Jill had been married longest, since high school. Jim and Betty had been married three years. Keith…well, Keith was still looking.

Bill was searching the WEB one night, and he hollered for Jill. "There is a place in Montana that has a house. I saved the page, come take a look!" he shouted with excitement. The listing read:

3 Bedrooms with 2 full baths.

Livingroom, kitchen, dining room shared. Computer and cell accessibility.

Nice outdoor area with ample parking.

If interested, call 000-000-0000 for Mr. Jeffrey.

"Now we have to get Jim and Betty on board!" exclaimed Bill.

"Oh, Betty would love it!" Jill jumped up

and down.

"Let's ask Keith too, all he ever does is rattle around that old house fixing stuff. It'll be good for him to get away," replied Bill.

"Okay, I'll call Betty!" Jill agreed. "You call Keith," she added with enthusiasm.

"Can't, Keith is on a grocery run," said Bill.

"Okay, call him afterwards. Betty is going to be over the moon!" said Jill.

Jill spoke to Betty for over an hour. Afterwards, she was so disappointed and plopped down on the couch beside Bill.

"What's wrong honey?" he asked.

"You know how excited we were for this trip?"

"Yes."

"Well, prepare for disappointment. Betty said she didn't see how they could go! They just laid out a bunch of cash for an entertainment center," replied Jill with a frown.

"All right, well--tell her to total up what they need, and what they have currently. Then have them call me tonight," said Bill.

"Sure thing. What should I tell her is the reason?" asked Jill.

"Well, I'll advance them the money against the Christmas bonus," he replied.

"Oh Bill, would you? I know why I married you! You are so wonderful, and I love you," said Jill, giving him a hug.

"I love you too," he replied.

****

Betty told Tim about the getaway.

 Tim said, "I don't know, can we afford it after buying the entertainment center?"

"I figured up the cost, sort-of an estimate. I'll go over it with you after you and Bill discuss it."

A few minutes later, the phone rang, and it was Bill.

"Hello Tim, it's Bill."

"How are you?" asked Tim.

"Look, I've been thinking. If you and Betty want to go, I'll lend you the money and can settle with the Christmas bonus," his friend offered.

"How much we talking?" asked Tim.

Bill gave Tim the figure.

"It sounds great to me, we're in!" said Tim.

All Bill had to do now was convince Keith.

I'll take a shower first, and think about what to say, he said to himself.

***

After his shower, Bill lifted up the receiver and called his friend. Keith picked up the phone after three rings.

"Hey Keith, how's it going?" asked Bill.

"Did you know, everything in this old house needs fixing? I'm sick of it," replied his friend tiredly.

"How'd you like to get away from that old house for a while?" said Bill with a chuckle.

"Great! You paying?" Keith laughed.

"No, but you can afford this," Bill countered.

"Well what is it?" asked Keith.

So Bill read Keith the ad.

"Keith, think of it--your own bed and private bath."

"Does this place have a TV?" asked Keith.

"Oh! Come on Keith! There's more to life than TV. Be adventurous--live life a little, bud!" Bill said. *Boy, my friend can sure be silly sometimes,* he thought to himself.

"All right, Bill. I'll bite--how much?" asked Keith.

Bill told Keith.

Keith said, "Yeah, I can swing that. When do you leave?"

"I have to call. I've been running around

trying to talk to you all. Oh, and Tim and Betty are going too!" explained Bill.

"Good, we can play cards!" said Keith hopefully. "Betty will opt out--that leaves four."

"Keith, don't you want to get back to nature, go on hikes, and smell the pine trees?" asked Bill.

***

The following day Bill called about the ad. The house was owned by an old woman, but when he called the telephone was answered by a male voice.

"The house is owned by my Aunt Amy, but I handle her affairs. I'm Jeffrey Mathers, but I'm called Mr. Jeffrey," said the man, his voice gentle, like a babbling brook.

"Oh I see! Well, we would like to book the cottage for two weeks," replied Bill hopefully.

"That sounds fine by me," said Mr. Jeffrey.

Bill gave him the information about him and his co-workers.

"For a small fee, I provide fresh linens, towels, and an 8 am wake-up call," offered Mr. Jeffrey.

"Fine, fine, thank you," said Bill.

"I'll see you on the first of next month. Good day, Bill," said the man.

"Thank you! Have a nice day."

***

Keith arrived at the airport first, bag in hand. He sat in the cafe for half an hour and had a coffee, killing time.

He mused--*I wonder who'll be late--Betty or Jill? Probably Jill.* Keith thought, chuckling to himself.

Just then Betty and Tim turned the corner by the bathrooms, and joined him in the cafe. Bill and Jill arrived 10 minutes later, as Keith predicted.

Then came the announcement over the airport speaker, loud and muffled as it always was. "Montana flight 334, boarding at gate three!"

Bill said to his friends, " If you're ready, let's board!"

The married couples had seats together, but Keith had a window seat next to a little dark haired girl. Keith said to the little girl, "Would you like to trade?"

The window seat always made him

nervous.

"Sure," said the little girl.

"Thanks!" Keith said, and they switched.

"I'm Keith," he said, introducing himself properly.

"My name is Kim, Kim Carter. That's my mom and brother!" she pointed to the seat in the front of them where a young woman and toddler sat.

"Mama's got her hands full right now, her name is Sue, and Ben is my brother!" the little girl prattled on.

"I think you are cute, Kim Carter!" exclaimed Keith.

"Kim Carter! You stop pestering that young man!" scolded Mrs. Carter.

Keith just laughed good naturedly.

"Do you have any friends in your

class?" Keith asked Kim.

"Oh, yes! Let's see…there's Mary, Trina, Christy, and Carol," she giggled, but then whispered, "But I really like Scott. Don't tell Mama!"

"Okay," Keith agreed. "Not a word. How old are you, Kim?"

"I'm eight and a half, and I'm in the third grade. How old are you?" She asked, with an excited squeal.

"Kim Carter!" came Mama's voice again, in a warning tone. "We don't go around asking nice young men their ages!"

"Yes, mama," Kim said.

"Oh no harm, Mrs. Carter. I'm 36."

"I go to Dave Wheder Elementary School in North Ridge," Kim chimed in again.

"My teacher's Ms. Lanter. She's so nice

and pretty. Everyone likes her! She gave me an ice cream once. Then there's my friend Christy--she has reddish hair and freckles. She makes me laugh, and Mama says we can play dolls at my house after we get back."

"That's really nice," said Keith, who didn't really know what to say.

"We're gonna get daddy. He's in the hospital because of the war, he broke his leg. Mama says when he mends we can have a big party," said Kim. Soon, she tired of talking and fell asleep. At this point, everyone could move around freely in the aircraft. Keith got up to walk around and stretch his legs.

Mrs. Carter and baby Ben on her hip came towards Keith in the aisle.

"Mr...I'm sorry, what did you say your

name was?"

"Keith," he replied.

"Mr. Keith, my husband is part of the Wounded Warrior Project. He didn't break his leg…" she bit her lip and fought tears which threatened to fall. "He was shot rescuing his buddy, and saved his life. You see, part of the leg splintered, and it may be months before it mends. I wouldn't want Kim to know he was shot. When he's better, we'll tell her," explained Mrs. Carter.

"Yes, but why tell me?" asked Keith, trying to understand.

"Because Kim dosen't know a stranger. If you ever see her again, remember now she is your friend," said Mrs. Carter. Keith replied, "I'll take all those I can get. Tell your husband I wish him well."

"Thank you, Mr. Keith," said the woman.

The *Fasten Your Seatbelt* signal came on, and everyone returned to their seats and buckled up.

As they landed, Kim woke up. "Keith, are we here? Can I see my Daddy?" she asked.

Keith replied, "Yes Kim, soon."

Mrs. Carter gathered their carry-ons and her children. They waved goodbye to Keith, and he waved back.

***

Mr. Jeffrey had sent a slinky silver limo and a friendly driver to greet them upon landing. The small group went to gather their luggage. They met the driver out front, and he loaded the luggage. The limo pulled away and into traffic. Soon they were crossing a bridge over a river. It criss-crossed across the land, not a bit in a straight line.

Trees sparkled beneath starry moonlight as birds drifted between waves of wind, and the skyline was majestically stormy.
"It's always as I imagined it. It's a marvel, beautiful dosen't begin to describe it," Keith said, gazing out the window sleepily and longing to dream.
"Let's go on an enchanted adventure," whispered Bill, and his friends smiled. They traveled through a forest of trees as tall as skyscrapers and in the distance blue mountains watched them from afar. The limo eventually wound

its way up then down below that mountain. In a small clearing, the driver stopped the limo and Mr. Jeffrey was there to meet them. He was small and wiry with shaggy black hair.

"I trust you had a nice flight?" he asked.

"Yes, it was very relaxing with fair weather all the way over," said Bill. The cottage was made of old wood and painted white. On the covered porch white wicker furniture with cushions awaited them beneath the swaying trees as storm clouds nestled high in the sky, visible even through night's blackness.

"You must be exhausted, let me show you to your rooms," said Mr. Jeffrey thoughtfully.

His aunt's house was charming inside,

and reflected the furniture style on the porch. She had decorated the home in a very tasteful way. Potted plants grew throughout the house, on windowsills, bookcases, counters, and tables. Soft colors of blue, cream, and peony danced through the rooms, taking various forms. Each piece of wicker furniture was well cushioned with softly accented pillows. The cottage had two floors, and the rooms were plenty. As the friends were shown around, they silently decided which bedrooms would be most suitable for them.

"Not to worry, there is plenty to do so you'll never be bored. There is a pool in the back garden, a horse stable within driving distance, and more. I took the liberty of drawing you a map. There are restaurants, coffee shops, and nightclubs in Lonesome Ridge, which is a town an hour away," explained Mr. Jeffrey, who left his map on the kitchen table.

Everyone thanked Mr. Jeffrey, who retired for the night. Tim and Betty were snacking in the kitchen, while Bill and Jill were unpacking. Keith flipped the television on and found a new episode of his favorite show, *Alone to watch.*

When everyone else was finished, they joined Keith in the living room.

Jim asked Keith, "Who ends up eating the bunny liver?"

Keith pointed towards the main character and said, "He does, I guess."

After *Alone* was over, everybody went

to their rooms while Keith unpacked and took a shower. Everyone was tired from the flight, so they slept soundly until morning came. At breakfast, the couples decided to go horseback riding. Keith opted out, and decided to go swimming. The water was a little cool, but it warmed by the afternoon. After swimming for hours, he stopped at a little restaurant for a burger and fries.

Everyone met back at the house that night. The couples were discussing what was on the agenda for the next day. Jill and Betty wanted to go shopping, and Bill and Tom wanted to go fishing.
Keith said, "Let's do something as a

group.”

“Okay Keith, what do you have in mind?” asked Bill.

“I’m not sure,” he replied.

As they pondered on this, Mr. Jeffrey came in with fresh towels.

“Hey Jeffrey--what else is there to do besides fishing?” asked Keith.

“Well, let’s see…there is a nice trail or two here if you like hiking,” said Mr. Jeffrey.

Everyone agreed it was a good idea, everyone but Keith that is.

Why did I have to open my big mouth? He chided himself.

“Come on Keith, it’s something everyone can do!” said Bill.

“Yeah, maybe we’ll take it easy on you, bud,” Tim laughed.

"*Fine,* but let's stay together…I'm not a nature crazed fellow," he sighed, giving in.

"We'll start at 10 am," said Jill.

"Let's make it 11, it's warmer by then. Is 11 okay everyone?" asked Betty, turning to the others.

"Sure, okay. We're in," said the guys. Keith was so *not* looking forward to this. Bugs, twigs in his hair, and sweltering humidity. Yeck! When he rose the next day, he sprayed all of his clothes with insect repellent. He decided it wouldn't hurt to spray them again, so he did. Keith got dressed, and sprayed bug repellent everywhere, even through his hair and on his hands.

After they breakfasted, they started out. Once the group had been walking for a while, they finally came to a trail where deer and other animals had trekked on their way to water.

Jill asked if there were any bears.

Betty said, "Hush, Jill. We've enough to deal with without worrying about that."

Bill and Tim chuckled. Keith stopped under a limb and got twigs in his hair. He was *so* mad. "Oh man! You have *got* to be kidding me!" he fussed, brushing at his hair.

They came to a fork in the road.

"Well, up or down?" Bill asked his friends.

"Downhill!" Keith yelled, because that was *precisely* how he felt his day was going.

"Yeah!" agreed everyone, a bit winded. So, they started downhill. They came across a log and a couple of chipmunks who ran, chattering as they went.

Betty screamed, "Oh my gosh! They scared the living daylights out of me!"

Up ahead was a structure of some kind sitting alone in a clearing.

"I don't believe it. It's a small farm in almost pristine condition!" exclaimed Bill.

"Somebody has taken really good care of it," said Tim.

"But who…and how'd they get back here to paint and manage it? Look, there's tire tracks!" said Bill.

The Irish in Keith came bubbling up and said, "Maybe it was spirits."

Everybody laughed. Bill and Jill went up to the door.

"Well what do you know? It's open!" said Jill. "Let's go in and look around." The others were hesitant. When about five minutes had passed, Jill hollered out,

"Betty--come on, you've gotta see this!" In the barn lay boxes stacked two and three high. They were quite wide as well, about four feet across. Betty began opening some of them. They were mostly full of clothes; hats, gloves, dresses, and more.

Keith stood in the doorway poised with awkward uncertainty.

Betty opened a box with a small chest in it. It was the size of a recipe box. She claimed this treasure as her own.

Jill opened a few more boxes. "More clothes," she said, with disappointment.

Bill and Tim joined the hunt for treasures.

Keith said, "Come on, let's go! We're going to get caught!"

Tim uncovered a hunting knife, and Bill found a cookie tin shaped like a log cabin in one of the boxes.

"Come on Keith, open one!" Bill encouraged.

"No way, man! I'm afraid someone's watching us!" Keith exclaimed worriedly.

Jill opened two more boxes, both filled with antique Christmas ornaments.

"They're so beautiful--I claim these!" she said with excitement.

"Come now Keith, just one box and we'll get off your case!" Betty said.

Keith grumbled, "Fine! Just one box and

then I think we should leave!"

He stomped over to a box and opened it.

"Okay, I got an envelope. Now let's go!" he snapped.

Everyone carted their treasures back through the forest. Upon getting back, they put everything in their rooms. Mr. Jeffrey came by again that afternoon with some more fresh towels.

"How much for those boxes out in the barn?" asked Bill.

"Mr. Bill, I assure you this house is the only structure on this property," he explained.

"Nah, seriously. When the trail forks and you go downhill----" Bill insisted.

"I'm quite certain this is the only structure on this land which follows the trail all the way to the creek," Mr.

Jeffrey interrupted.

That night, the friends all opened and explored their treasures. Betty had an old cookie recipe she made them that night. They were delicious! Everyone said they would melt in your mouth. Later on, she sold the cookies at the supermarket and made a lot of money. Jill sold her Christmas decorations and ornaments to a collector, which brought a handsome profit. When Keith opened his envelope, he found a bearer bond worth $500,000 dollars. Everybody packed up and left Montana.

On the plane home, Keith sat down behind an injured man. When the Fasten Your Seatbelt sign came on, they were allowed to walk around. A little girl came up and grabbed his hand.

Keith looked startled, for there stood Kim Carter.

She said, "Hi Keith! Come meet my daddy."

It turned out that he was the man sitting in front of Keith the whole time. Keith and Carter hit it off right from the start, so much in fact, that he helped Carter and his family get a house. It was down the street from the new house Keith bought for himself. Kim, who didn't know a stranger, became great friends with Keith, who had four new dear friends to add to the group.

About the Author

Mary lives outside of a quiet little town in Northern Kentucky. She is laid back and witty. She grew up in the beautiful hills of Kentucky. Mary enjoys life with her sister, and Socks the cat.